Sammy's Hiding Place

Little Stinker Series
Book 9

Dave Sargent was born and raised on a dairy farm in northwest Arkansas. When he began writing in 1990, he made a decision to dedicate the remainder of his life to encouraging children to read and write. He is very good with students and teachers alike. He and his wife Pat travel across the United States together. They write about animals with character traits. They are good at showing how animals act a lot like kids.

Sammy's Hiding Place

Little Stinker Series
Book 9

By Dave Sargent

Illustrated by Elaine Woodward

Ozark Publishing, Inc.
P.O. Box 228
Prairie Grove, AR 72753

Cataloging-in-Publication Data

Sargent, Dave, 1941–
    Sammy's hiding place / by Dave Sargent ;
illustrated by Elaine Woodward. —Prairie
Grove, AR : Ozark Publishing, c2007.
        p. cm. (Little stinker series ; 9)

    "Be resourceful"—Cover.
    SUMMARY: Sammy creates havoc at
school but gets home safely.
        ISBN 1-59381-297-3 (hc)
                1-59381-298-1 (pbk)

    1. Skunks—Juvenile fiction.
2. Dogs—Juvenile fiction.
[1. Games—Fiction.]
I. Woodward, Elaine, 1956– ill.
II. Title. III. Series.

        PZ7.S243Sa 2007
        [Fic]—dc21   2005906114

Printed in the United States of America

Inspired by

the day I hid Sammy in the teacher's closet.

Dedicated to

all children who would love to take a skunk to school.

Foreword

When Sammy crawled into a toe sack full of leaves, he fell asleep. Dave took the leaves to school. When Dave finds the little skunk, he hides it in the teacher's closet.

Contents

If you'd like to have Dave Sargent, the author of the Little Stinker Series, visit your school free of charge, call: 1-800-321-5671.

One

School Is Out!

When I discovered Sammy in the sack of leaves I took to school, I hid him in the teacher's closet. I knew he would curl up in a ball and go to sleep. He always slept all day.

The teacher gently rang the bell on her desk for recess. We closed our books and put them away. Then we quietly walked outside.

Once outside everyone began screaming and yelling at the top of their lungs. It seemed to me that recess was over before it started. The teacher was ringing her bell. This time it wasn't a gentle ring. It was a hard ring. Why, that bell could be heard for a hundred miles!

We ran to the steps and lined up, then walked quietly back to the room. Everyone sat at their desk and waited for instructions from the teacher.

The teacher walked to the closet in the back of the room. She said, "We're going to make decorations for Thanksgiving."

She opened the closet door and took out some colored paper. But the rattle of the paper woke Sammy. I had a terrible feeling. I just knew something bad was about to happen.

Sure enough, just as the teacher began pushing the door shut with her foot, Sammy stuck his head out.

The door caught Sammy behind the front legs. The teacher looked down to see why the door didn't close. When she saw Sammy, she threw her hands in the air and screamed bloody murder!

Papers flew everywhere! The teacher's scream scared the kids half to death. They began screaming, then ran out the door and down the hall.

Two

Find That White Varmint

I didn't know what to do. I knew I was in a whole lot of trouble. I grabbed Sammy and crawled out of the window. It was a long way to the ground. I jumped anyway.

I landed in the shrubs next to the building. I stuck Sammy behind the shrubs. I crawled out, brushed myself off and ran around the school to where the other kids were.

By the time I got around the building, all the teachers and kids were outside. Everyone had heard the screaming and had come running. I never saw so much confusion.

The principal settled everyone down and then tried to find out what had happened.

Well, as it turned out no one really saw Sammy except the teacher. She had never seen a white skunk so she didn't know that it was a skunk. She told the principal that it was a white varmint of some kind.

School let out while the high school boys and some of the teachers searched the building for a white varmint. I just stood there. I never uttered a word.

I knew Sammy would be okay where I put him. He didn't like light. I figured he would just curl up and go to sleep again. I would worry about him later.

Three

Sammy Goes Home

It was way after lunchtime before the principal decided it was safe to go back inside the school. Everyone was still excited. Some were even scared. Most were happy because there was no school work for the rest of the day.

When we went out for afternoon recess, I got my toe sack. While the other kids were playing, I broke some twigs off of the trees around the school house. I knew that if I was going to take Sammy home, I would have to put something in the sack with him.

After filling the sack part way full with twigs, I went to where I had left Sammy. There was no one on the back side of the school building. The kids never played around back. I put Sammy in the sack with the twigs and left it there.

When school was out, I ran behind the school house and grabbed my toe sack with Sammy inside. I hurried to the bus, climbed on and went to the back. All the way home I held the top of the toe sack tight. I wasn't taking any chances.

On that day, I figured I must be the luckiest person on the face of the earth. I got off the bus and made it home without anyone knowing that Sammy had been to school.

Four

Skunk Facts

Skunks use leaves and grass to line their den. In wintertime they make a big ball using grass. They put the ball in the opening of their den to keep out the cold.